WHAT'S THAT NOISE?

written by **Michelle Edwards** and **Phyllis Root**

illustrated by **Paul Meisel**

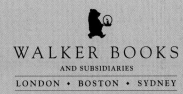

WALKER BOOKS
AND SUBSIDIARIES
LONDON · BOSTON · SYDNEY

"Sleep tight," said Mummy to Alex
and his little brother, Ben.

"Don't let the bedbugs bite," said Daddy.

"We won't," said Alex softly.

It was quiet in the hallway.
Quiet in the room. Quiet all around.

WHOOSH WHOOSH WHOOSH! went the night noises.
WHOOSH WHOOSH WHOOSH!

Ben sat up. "Alex," he whispered, "what's that noise?"

"Nothing," said Alex. "I'm tired. Go to sleep."

AROO AROO AROO!
went the night noises.

"Alex, I'm scared," said Ben.
"Will you sing me a song?"

"Just go to sleep," said Alex.

"*Please* will you sing me a song?" said Ben.

"Oh, all right," said Alex. "Just one song."

HOO HOO HOO!
went the night noises.

"Sing it in my bed," said Ben.

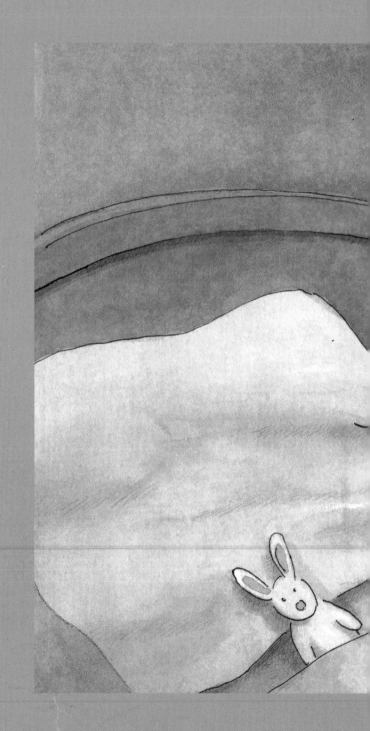

Alex looked across the room.

Ben's bed was far away across the cold, dark floor.

Alex didn't like to put his feet down on cold floors in dark rooms.

Something might grab his feet. Something might bite his toes.

A foot-grabbing, toe-biting something that went WHOOSH AROO HOO!

Alex hugged his bear tight.

"I'll sing it in my bed," said Alex. "OK?"

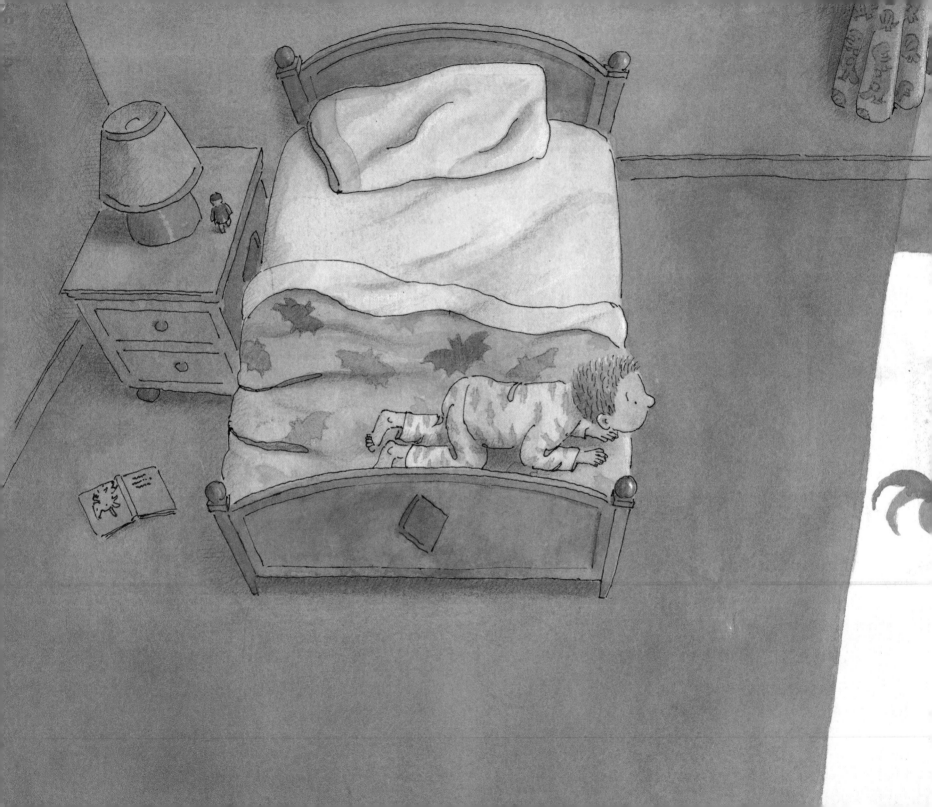

But Ben didn't answer.

"Ben?" asked Alex.

Ben still didn't answer.

The room was very dark. Alex couldn't see Ben.

The room was very quiet. Alex couldn't hear Ben's noisy breathing.

Where was Ben?

Alex jumped out of bed.

Thud! went his feet on the cold floor.

Alex leaped across the room. His toes barely touched the floor.

Alex pulled Ben's covers back.

There was Ben!

"You were here all along," said Alex.

"Yes," said Ben. "Now will you sing me a song?"

"OK," said Alex. He got into Ben's bed, pulled the covers up around them both and sang,

"WHOOSH! goes the wind.

AROO! goes a dog.

HOO! goes a baby owl."

"HOO, HOO, HOO!"

sang Ben.

Alex and Ben sang until the
night noises all went away.

And it was quiet in the hallway.
Quiet in the room. Quiet all around.

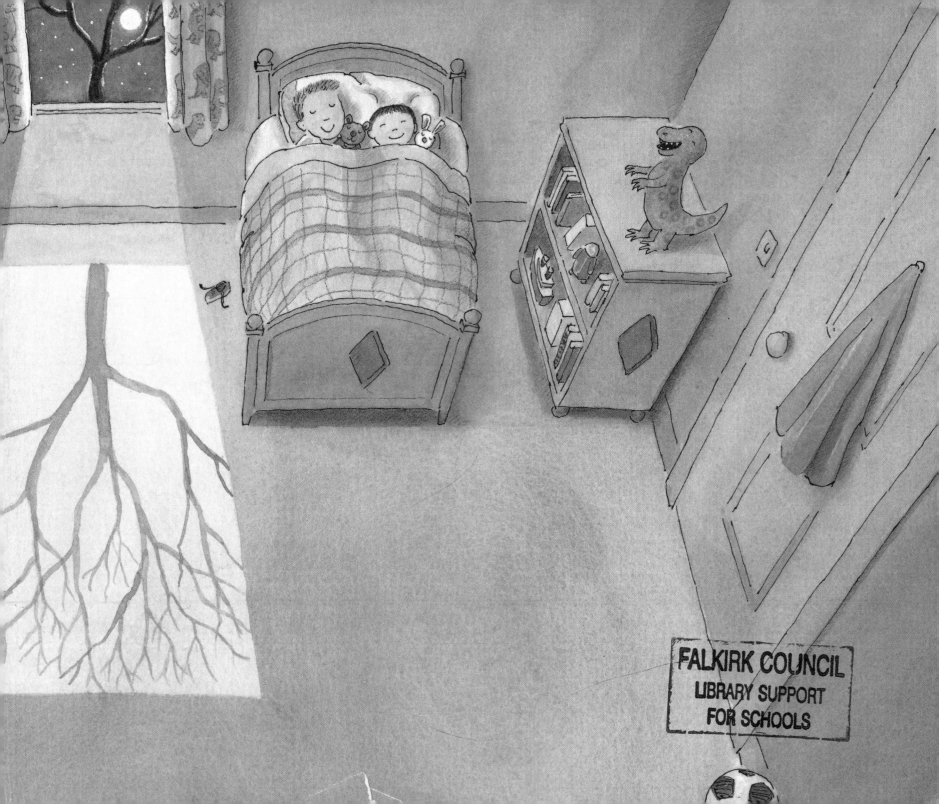

With love to the memory of Emily Crofford,
a good writer and a good friend
M.E. and P.R.

For my sons – Peter, Alex and Andrew
P.M.

First published 2002 by Walker Books Ltd
87 Vauxhall Walk, London SE11 5HJ

2 4 6 8 10 9 7 5 3 1

Text © 2002 Michelle Edwards and Phyllis Root
Illustrations © 2002 Paul Meisel

This book has been typeset in ITC Highlander

Printed in China

British Library Cataloguing in Publication Data:
a catalogue record for this book is
available from the British Library

ISBN 0-7445-8040-4

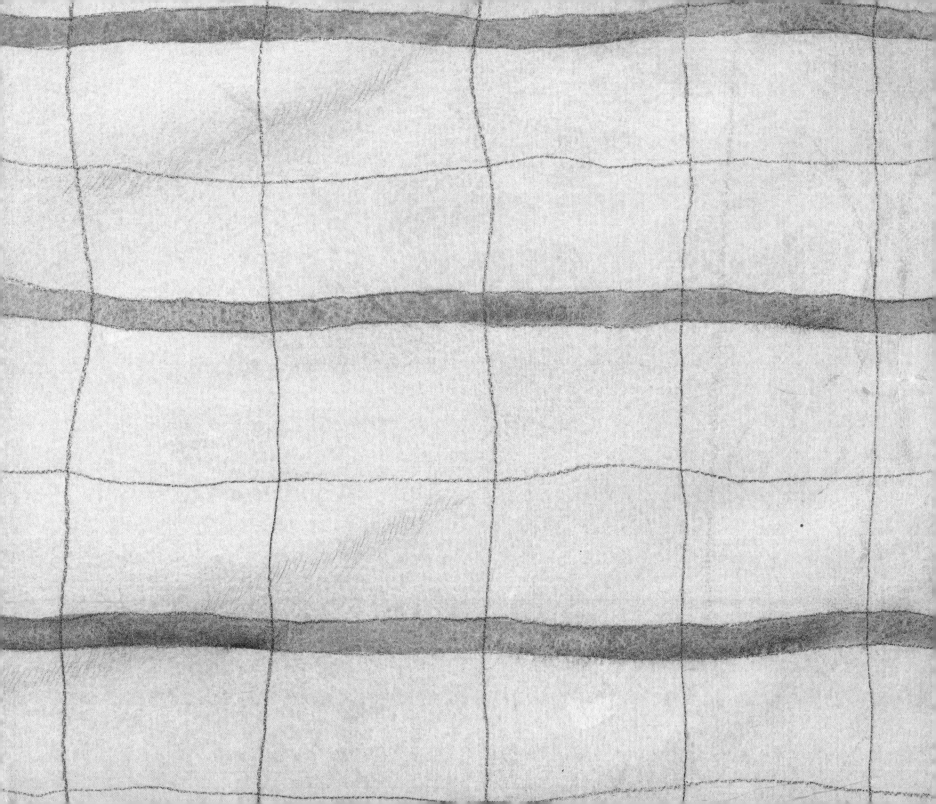

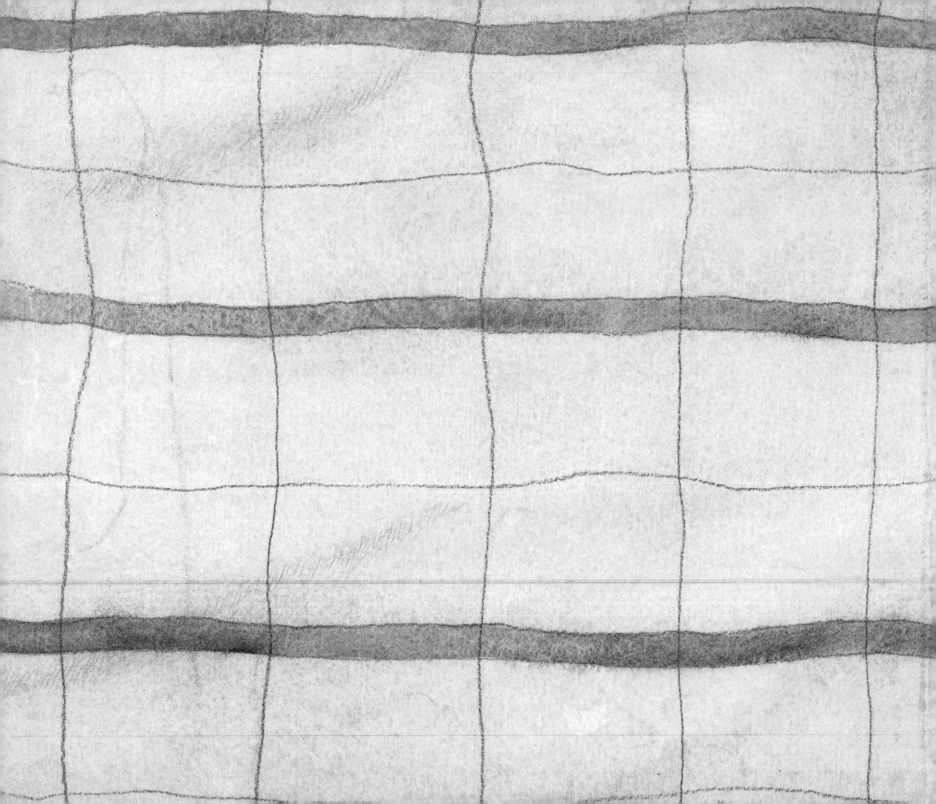